Book Uncle and Me

Book Uncle and Me

·

Uma Krishnaswami

Illustrations by JULIANNA SWANEY

Groundwood Books
House of Anansi Press
Toronto   Berkeley

Text copyright © 2016 by Uma Krishnaswami
Published in Canada and the USA in 2016 by Groundwood Books
Original edition published by Scholastic India Pvt. Ltd. in 2012

Groundwood Books / House of Anansi Press
groundwoodbooks.com

We acknowledge for their financial support of our publishing program
the Canada Council for the Arts, the Ontario Arts Council and
the Government of Canada.

Canada Council   Conseil des Arts
for the Arts   du Canada

ONTARIO ARTS COUNCIL
CONSEIL DES ARTS DE L'ONTARIO

an Ontario government agency
un organisme du gouvernement de l'Ontario

With the participation of the Government of Canada | Canadä
Avec la participation du gouvernement du Canada

Library and Archives Canada Cataloguing in Publication
Krishnaswami, Uma, author
Book Uncle and me / Uma Krishnaswami ; pictures by
Julianna Swaney.
Issued also in print and electronic formats.
ISBN 978-1-55498-808-2 (bound).—ISBN 978-1-55498-810-5
(html).—ISBN 978-1-55498-811-2 (mobi)
I. Swaney, Julianna, illustrator II. Title.
PZ7.K75Bo 2016   j813'.54   C2015-908444-X
C2015-908445-8

Jacket design by Michael Solomon
Jacket art by Julianna Swaney

Groundwood Books is committed to protecting our natural environment.
As part of our efforts, the interior of this book is printed on paper that
contains 100% post-consumer recycled fibers, is acid-free and is processed
chlorine-free.

Printed and bound in Canada

To young readers everywhere

1

The Right Book

WATCH ME ZIGZAG after school, every single afternoon, between the bus stop and Horizon Apartment Flats. It's where my best friend Reeni lives in 3B and I live in 3A.

Reeni and I wave to our friend Anil. He karate-blocks and punches at us through the bus window. It's his way to say *Good-bye, see you tomorrow.*

The bus pulls off down the road.

"Bye, Yasmin," says Reeni.

"Bye, Reeni," I say.

She turns to go home. I go zig-zig-zag, off on my daily mission.

Mind the crooked tree. Mind the istri lady with her iron and heap of clothes. Mind the broken pavement and the pigeons cooling their feathers in mud puddles. Watch-watch-watch …

And here it is! Book Uncle's Lending

Library on the corner of St. Mary's Road and 1st Cross Street, with books spread out on planks of wood and a small tin can for donations, just to help out, if anyone wants to.

Here is the sign in faded old letters:

Books. Free.
Give one.
Take one.
Read–Read–Read.

Perfect!

In all of India, could there be a better corner lending library than this?

2

Number One Patron

"Hello, Yasmin-ma," says Book Uncle. "How's my Number One Patron?"

I don't know about Number One, but I'm sure I am Book Uncle's busiest patron, as I mean to read one book every day. Every single day, forever. I started last year right after I turned eight. That already feels like a billion years ago, because now I am past four hundred. Books, I mean.

I return yesterday's floppy paperback. Book Uncle beams at me through glasses so fat they make his eyes extra big and extra smiley.

"Did you like it?" he asks. He really wants to know.

"Of course," I say. I always do. I always like the books he gives me.

He waves at the piles. "Take another, take another. Something different this time?"

He points to a thin book with a dark green cover.

I take a look. It seems a little skinny.

I pick it up. I open it. And for the first time ever, in all the time I've been getting books from Book Uncle, I am not sure.

"It looks too easy," I say.

"Short and sweet," says Book Uncle. "Old Indian story. You can read it three times in a day if you like."

I turn the book over and then over again.

"I can read bigger books," I say.

Book Uncle looks at me sideways. He opens his mouth as if there is something he wants to say. Then he closes it again as if he has changed his mind.

Finally, when I think maybe he has forgotten I'm still there, he says, very softly, "Right book for the right person for the right day. As you know well, that is my motto."

He's right. It is. It's a good motto. He has always given me the right book on the right day, hasn't he?

"I'll take it," I tell him.

I waste no time. As soon as I have stepped over the broken bits of pavement (which I really wish the city would fix so I could walk and read without worrying about where to put my feet), I start to read the book.

And I am sorry to say that I was right. It is a story for little kids, about a king of doves who gets himself and all his followers stuck in a trap set by a hunter.

At first I'm disappointed, but then I

think I'll keep going. Might as well find out what happens to those doves.

There they are, caught in a net! I turn-turn-turn the pages. No escape, no escape. Try-try-try. Still no escape.

Will they save themselves?

Hmm. This may be a book for little kids, but still, it's giving me something to think about. It drives me crazy when a book does that.

All the way up the stairs to 3A, I worry about those doves.

I read the dove book once straight through, after homework and dinner, and I find out that the dove king and all his followers do get free! I know, I know. I'm giving away the ending. But here's the thing. The point of a story is not the ending. The point is, What does it *mean*?

While I'm still wondering about that, my father calls me to see something on TV.

3

Swirling T-shirts

"It's a T-shirt-folding contest," Wapa says. He makes room for me on the sofa.

"They fold T-shirts?"

"They do. Have you ever heard of such a thing?"

"Wapa," I say, "why would anyone want to take part in a T-shirt-folding contest?"

"See for yourself," he says. "There are all kinds of crazy people in this crazy world, my Minu."

My mother laughs. "Including those who sit around watching those crazy people fold T-shirts."

A whistle tweets. A dozen people on TV make a dozen rainbow-colored piles of T-shirts, their hands flying as fast as Anil's karate punches. It makes me dizzy to watch those swirling T-shirts. The room spins around me and the air is full of T-shirts and there is no ground under my feet anymore.

I gasp and clutch at the sofa. Wapa pats me on the shoulder and the room steadies.

The whistle blows again. Everyone stops.

The winner has folded thirty T-shirts in sixty seconds. That is only two seconds per T-shirt.

"That is fast," I say, able to breathe again.

"Blink of an eye," says Wapa.

How long would it take me to do a thing like that? Many, many blinks, I think. Which reminds me of those doves and their king and the hunter. Where were these T-shirt-folding people with their flying hands when the doves needed help?

Wait. That is in a story and this ... is real? Give me a story any day.

Umma says, "You people want to practice folding clothes? There's a whole clothesline full on the terrace."

Wapa turns off the TV. The phone rings.

"I'll get it," he says. He picks up the receiver with a cheery "Hello!" But in a minute his face changes, so I know who that is.

When he hangs up, he says, "You know who that was."

Wapa's big brother, Rafiq Uncle, always has that effect on us.

"He's coming to visit us?" asks Umma.

Wapa nods. "But he's coming on business. Maybe he'll be so busy he won't have time to criticize."

My mother shakes her head, as if she knows that Rafiq Uncle will always have time for a few well-chosen words to put her in her place. She goes into a flurry of worrying about all the things in the flat that will need to be dusted and mopped and polished. Suddenly the only tube of toothpaste we have left, squeezed half empty, that wasn't even a problem until now, becomes just another sign of her bad housekeeping.

"I'll get some more," Wapa says. He escapes, leaving me to the mercy of Umma's duster.

4

Just a Slogan

THAT DUSTER IS a weapon. Umma uses it against dust, clutter and all signs of untidiness. I retreat to my room, which is what you might call a strategic move. Just in case she takes it into her head that I need to be dusted off, too.

In the safety of my room, I try to make sense of things. Something is bothering me about that book, and it's not just the story.

It's Book Uncle, I decide. Why did he give me that funny look before he handed me that book? As if he would like to say something but couldn't find the words. He seemed distracted. That's it. As if something was on his mind.

Is something wrong? Maybe I am just worrying for no reason.

I turn to the story in the hope that I can unravel its puzzle. How strange that such a skinny book can leave so many questions in my mind. I flip the pages to see if maybe there was something I missed.

Doves. King. Trapped in a net. Hunter. Get help. Get free. The end.

"So what?" I say out loud.

"So what about what?" says Umma, brandishing the duster over my head.

"Help!" I say. "I surrender."

"No need, silly girl," says Umma. "How about you help me instead?" She points to a pile of books on the floor by my bed. Then she points to the shelf.

"Get my drift?" she says.

"Umma," I tell her. "I get your drift. I get it fine."

We get to work. She whisks the duster over my shelf. I put the books away. While I do that, I tell her the story of the doves and the hunter.

"That's an old Indian story," Umma says.

"I know. Book Uncle told me. But Umma, what's the big lesson in it? For me, I mean?"

"I can't tell you that," she says. "I can tell you what something means for me. How can I tell you what it means for you? Only you can know that."

I tell her about Book Uncle's motto. Right book, right person, right day.

"So why was this such a great book for me?"

"That's just a slogan," she says. "Right book and all that. He just likes to say that. Don't take it too literally."

"What does that mean?"

"Taking something literally?"

"Yes."

"As if every word of it is true," she says. "You know, it's just a catchy slogan. It gets more people to pick up a book. Nothing wrong with that. Don't take it too seriously."

Then Umma looks around my room, nods her head and moves on with her duster to the next target.

Too literally? Too seriously? Is that how I'm taking it? Is it just a slogan?

I don't think so. I think Book Uncle really does find the right book for the right person. On the right day. That I am pretty sure about.

Before I can arrive at any conclusions, Wapa comes back with enough toothpaste to polish up the teeth of the entire Indian army.

5

Hiya!

AND SO THE weekend gets dusted off. On Monday we're off to school again, which is just the way things are, one day after the next after the next. It's a bit like folding T-shirts, when you think about it. Folding-folding-folding is not so different from wheels turning-turning-turning.

The bus driver honks his horn. He sticks his head out of the window and yells at a man on a bike.

"You think you own the road or what?"

The man on the bike yells back, "You think you run the city?"

"Hey, Yasmin," says Reeni. "Look at that!" She points at something outside the bus window.

I look where she's pointing, but I don't see anything so great, and anyway, I am still all tangled up in slogans and taking things literally. Maybe I am taking the dove story too literally, as if every word is true. Maybe instead I should be looking for some other meaning in it. What have I missed in that story?

"You missed it," Reeni says.

"Are you reading my mind?" I ask her in surprise. "I was thinking maybe I didn't get it but how did you know that?"

Now Reeni looks puzzled.

"Get what? What are you talking about? I was trying to show you the poster for the new Karate Samuel movie."

"Is that all?" I say. "I thought you were going to help me work out the story in this book."

"How can I help you work out the story in your book when I haven't even read it?" Reeni says.

"Reeni, you can't read it," I say. "I have to give it back. Today. Remember? I'm reading one book every day —"

"Fine," she says. "Don't share. You never share."

"I do," I protest. "I share a desk with you in school. I share this seat with you in the bus and when you come over I share ..."

I stop to think what it is I share.

"Everything," I end up.

Reeni gives me the kind of look that tells me she is not impressed.

"You should see Karate Samuel's round kicks," says Anil. He is trying to change the subject to stop Reeni and me from arguing. I don't like it, either, but who started it? Not me.

"Karate Samuel is just a movie star,"

I say, turning pages. But now the words are bumping up and down. The bus has turned under the flyover by Gemini Studio and is going *gada-gadaa* over the potholes, past the circle where the lights have stopped working and a policeman is dancing around, trying to control traffic.

"Hiya!" Anil's karate hands fly past my face, quick-block punching. I manage to catch the dove book before it falls down.

"Stop it," I tell him. "Have you lost your marbles?" The minute the words are out I wish I could take them back but it's too bad, because you can't hit Delete that way.

Anil looks puzzled, so I rush to explain. "Not real marbles. It means, Don't be crazy."

Now I want to hit Delete-delete-delete, and I can't. What have I done? Will Anil be upset because I called him crazy? I don't want both my friends to be angry with me.

But Anil only says, "What's wrong with being a little crazy? It's fun!" And he trades air-punches with the boy sitting across the aisle.

"Birdie, little birdie, do you know my sad story?" the bus driver sings as we turn into the schoolgrounds.

Is he singing about those doves?

No, he seems to be singing a sad song because he is happy, which makes no sense at all.

6

Word List

Mrs. Rao is walking up and down between the desks. She is keeping an eye on things.

Just my luck, she catches me sneaking a quick peek into the dove book to see if I can find whatever it is I'm missing.

"Yasmin," says Mrs. Rao. "Will you please put that book away and work on your word list."

Are word lists more important than me searching for important clues? More important than reading?

"Mrs. Rao, ma'am," I say. "I'm just reading."

"Not now, Yasmin," she says. "I know you like to read —"

"I do!" I say. "I've read more than four hundred books in the last —"

But Mrs. Rao does not want to hear about my reading marathon.

"Don't interrupt me, Yasmin." She is now interrupting me and how is that all right? "I want you to work on your word list now," she says. "I want you to use those words in sentences."

I give up.

"Yes, ma'am," I say, and now I am staring at the word list trying to make sense out of it.

Sometimes the words on Mrs. Rao's lists share vowels. *Ground. Proud. Aloud. Resound.* Sometimes they share consonants. *Flower. Fleeting. Flamingo.*

This is one weird list. These words don't seem to share anything.

Plan. Election. City. Office.

I stare at the words until they begin to fly around before my eyes as if they are birds flapping their wings.

31

Reeni nudges me and nearly makes me drop my notebook.

"Write your sentences," she whispers.

"Okay," I whisper back. Is school not supposed to be a place where you learn to think? Nobody is letting me think today.

Reeni lets out a hissy sound as if she is — what's the word?

Exasperated, that's what. With me.

"Yasmin, Reeni," says Mrs. Rao, who now looks exasperated with both of us.

"Yes, Mrs. Rao," we say together.

Reeni starts to write. She writes fast. From the corner of my eye I can see Anil getting to work. He is writing slowly, but he is writing.

I'd better start writing, too. So I do, letting those words fly around my head in circles.

This is how they come out on the paper:

The king of doves and all his subjects are caught in a net. Who will get them out? Quick, make a plan! Call everyone in the city. Don't sit there in your office. Hold an election. Help!

Mrs. Rao walks between the desks again and now she is looking over our shoulders and she is reading, reading.

"That's … very interesting," says Mrs. Rao when she gets to me. "What does it mean?"

How did I know she would ask me that? I have no idea. The words just came out that way.

7

Posters

I THINK ABOUT Mrs. Rao's words all day. *Plan. Election. City. Office.* And I think about my words, too, the words in my letter. I am still thinking about them on the way home from school.

Looking out the bus window, I see something. I see the movie poster that Reeni and Anil tried to show me before, when I was too busy reading my book.

Only it is not a movie poster.

"That's an election poster," I say.

"It is?" says Reeni. "You're right. It looks like it. But that's Karate Samuel. What's a movie star like him doing on an election poster?"

"Movie stars run in elections all the time," I say. "Don't you know anything?"

Reeni stares at me. Suddenly I hear the words I have just spoken as if they are echoing all around us in the bus.

Don't you know anything? Anything? Anything ... thing ... thing?

Oh, those words! I didn't mean to say them. Well, maybe I did mean to say them, but not that way. I didn't mean them to be mean. They flew out of my mouth on careless wings and I wish-wish-wish that I could take them back.

But it's too late. Reeni has heard them already.

She says, "Fine. You know everything, don't you, Miss Yasmingenius?"

Anil rolls his eyes and makes little punching gestures at me. I wish he had really punched me. Before I said those words. But what can I do now? It's too late.

Umma says sometimes it's good to think twice before you speak. Sometimes I forget to think even once.

It never used to matter with Reeni. I could say anything to Reeni and it would be all right.

Suddenly it matters, and I don't know what has changed.

The traffic is so busy now that the bus can only go very, very slowly. The driver is not happy this afternoon. He does not sing. Instead he honks his horn. He yells at cars, scooters, autorickshaws, other buses and even a man driving a herd of goats across the road. The goats don't know about traffic lights, so the bus has to wait until they all cross.

While we wait I notice something that I could have pointed out to Reeni, if she was still speaking to me, that is.

People are slapping posters on walls and lampposts. They are slapping posters on everything they can find. I'm sure if I was standing still, reading by the side of the road, they would slap a poster on me.

That is a lot of people all wanting to be mayor. Every poster has a logo for all the different parties the candidates belong to — a hand, a wheel, a tree, a star, a hammer and sickle, a camel and more.

This is going to be a crazy busy election.

"The star! That's Karate Samuel's party," Anil says.

"Of course," says Reeni. "He *is* a star."

She's talking to Anil, I see, but not to me. There is a row of posters with the picture of the present mayor, S. L. Yogaraja, telling everyone to reelect him. Mayor S.L.Y. Some people say his initials suit him fine.

Other candidates have posters in clumps here and there, urging us to vote for them. Well, not us. Not kids. I have never understood why they don't let kids vote. This is another thing I would like to discuss with my friends, but I can't exactly talk to them about anything right now.

Karate Samuel has lots and lots of posters. He is leaping and punching and kicking all over his posters. His posters scream in giant letters: BEST CANDI-DATE! A-ONE HERO!

Strings of Karate Samuel's posters hang between the trees on both sides of the road, like flapping lines of washing. They get smaller and smaller as our bus goes faster.

It would be exciting, if only Reeni was excited along with me.

But Reeni is wearing a frown on her face.

I swallow my words. I say nothing.

8

Hello, Everyone

I RETURN THE dove book to Book Uncle.

"Did you like it?" he asks.

"It was … interesting," I say. "But why was it so perfect for me?"

I don't mean to sound ungrateful, but I can't help myself. I am puzzled and it just comes bursting out that way.

"Ah," he says. "That is a very good question."

"Thank you," I say. "But what is the answer?"

"Sometimes you have to let the perfect book sit in your mind for a while before it begins to mean something." He hands me two more books. "One for now, one for later."

When I thank him, he smiles and nods at me, his Number One Patron.

That afternoon my mother gets ready to go shopping. She has cleaned the house until she is satisfied that it is spotless and ready for Rafiq Uncle's visit. Now we need to buy vegetables and fruits, so he will not think for a minute that we don't eat properly. Our usual bunch of bananas and enough veggies for a quick curry will not do.

Umma picks up her purse and shopping bags.

"Come on, Yasmin," she says. "Let's go."

As the door of our flat clicks shut behind us, the one across the hall flies open. That's Reeni's flat, 3B. Out comes Shoba Aunty, Reeni's mother. We say hello to her but she barely nods back. She seems to be in a big hurry. She must be on her way to the TV station to work the evening shift.

On the way downstairs we say hello to Chinna Abdul Sahib of 2B who has popped out to look in his mailbox. He nods back, which is more than he usually does.

Chinna Abdul Sahib is a drummer. He plays a big round ghatam made of clay. He is in big demand to play that clay pot-drum at concerts and weddings. Wapa says it takes a lot of strength to play that kind of drum. I wonder if that is why Chinna Abdul Sahib wastes no energy talking.

We say hello to the newly married couple in 1B. They are standing outside their door, admiring the new doorbell that the electrician has just fixed. They say hello together. Then they look at each other as if they have never seen such a beautiful sight before.

We say hello to the electrician.

We say hello to the flower seller who is just arriving, and to the istri lady in her little booth downstairs. She's filling her big heavy iron with hot coals so she can press and fold the clothes of all her customers in Horizon Apartment and the neighboring flats.

"Can I put some money in Book Uncle's tin?" I ask.

"Hurry," says Umma.

I run over to Book Uncle. My coins clink in his tin.

"Thank you," he says.

We cross the road.

"You're very quiet," Umma says.

"Mmm," I say.

"Is something wrong?" she asks.

I mumble, "No. Not really." But my voice sounds guilty, as if it's trying to escape from telling a total lie because maybe something is not wrong, exactly, but it's not exactly right, either. How can everything be right when my best friend Reeni has gone all huffy and quiet and it's all my fault?

"How are you?" says the fruit man, when we get to his stand with rows of fruit all neatly stacked. "I have nice bananas and guavas for you."

Umma picks her fruit — guavas that are green on top but they will be pink inside when we cut them open, and tiny bananas from the hills. The man puts them all in a bag and hands the bag to Umma. The guavas settle to the bottom, with the bunches of little bananas on top. They all jiggle into place, just the way a perfect book settles in my mind.

Something roars behind me.

"Yasmin, watch out!" says Umma.

Just in time, I leap out of the way.

9

The Important Things

THE BIG BLUE van rattles past. Its horn shrieks.

Another second and I would have been mango pulp. Guava jelly.

"Yasmin," Umma scolds, "don't give me a heart attack! Always with your head in the clouds, always wrapped up in your own thoughts. What will I do with you?"

The fruit man's wife clucks at me from her veggie stand next to his. She waves her hand to let me know that I should step off the road and onto the broken pavement, which I do.

I am not always wrapped up in my own thoughts, I want to say. But I don't say it, because Umma is the one wrapped up now in worry. She is wearing a big blanket of worry that has to do with Rafiq Uncle and how his visits always give Wapa a headache.

That roar again. The van is back!

"Be careful," warns the fruit man. "Nothing better to do — these political heroes of ours and their election campaign people. They don't care about election issues. They think life is nothing but one big TV screen."

The van pulls up, slows down. It has two big posters like a tent on its roof. Karate Samuel is kicking and punching all over those posters as if he is doing his karate demo to the very loud music from the van's speakers.

Over the music, the driver shouts, "Want a tip-top mayor? Vote for Karate Samuel!"

"What'll he do for me?" the fruit man shouts back.

"And me?" his wife pipes up from her vegetable stand. She picks up an onion and tosses it in one hand, as if she's practicing. As if any minute she will throw it at Karate Samuel's poster.

The driver only yells as he drives off, "A-One hero! Karate Samuel for mayor!"

"Who are you going to vote for?" I ask my mother.

"I don't know," says Umma.

"What about him?" I point after the van. It has now sped through a red light and is quickly vanishing into the traffic.

"That cinema-kaaran?" says Umma. "Why should I vote for him?"

"Just asking," I say. She's right. He is a cinema guy. But is that a problem?

"They all want votes," says the fruit man. "Then when they get elected, they don't *do* anything."

That is a problem. Because grown-ups are supposed to keep their promises, aren't they?

We buy onions and potatoes and bitter melon from the fruit man's wife.

"I don't like bitter melon," I say.

Umma buys it anyway. She needs to show Rafiq Uncle that she is no slouch in the kitchen and that she can make traditional dishes. She does not say this but I know. The vegetable lady fills our second bag and hands it to me. I grab it with both hands. It is heavy.

Then we walk home.

"Umma," I ask as I drag the bag full of veggies up the stairs. "What is an election issue?"

"The things that people care about," says Umma, jiggling the key in the keyhole. She pushes the door open with her shoulder. "The candidates' positions on things."

"What things?"

"You know, important things." She waves her hand as if the important things will appear in our flat and walk across our floor. "Things that political leaders have to manage."

"Does Mayor SLY manage important things?" I ask.

She tries to be serious. "Uh … ye-e-es, I suppose he …" Then she laughs at the silly name that everyone calls the mayor, because really, it fits him so well. "I don't know, Minu. I don't trust him, either."

10

The Permit

I MANAGE TO finish one of the two books that Book Uncle gave me. It is a mystery — the kind of book you can read in one big gulp and it does not feel like work. Not like that dove book. Skinny as that one was, its story is still flapping around in my mind.

The second Book Uncle book is a karate book. I'll read it later and then maybe I'll pass it on to Anil.

In the morning, before I catch the bus to school, I decide to return the mystery book. That way I can get a new one.

I'm thinking I'd like to give a book to

Reeni, too, but she's not interested in karate. Maybe Book Uncle can find me a
book Reeni would like. Something about
animals or movies. Reeni is crazy about
animals, the bigger the better. She's only a
little less crazy about movies.

Oh, she is a crazy girl, my friend Reeni,
and I want her back. I want her not to be
angry with me anymore.

I'm busy tossing all these thoughts
around in my mind, but then I get to the
corner. The istri lady is yelling at her son.
The buses are rattling down the road. It
seems like a normal morning. But is it?

Because what I see stops me cold.

Book Uncle's place looks different.
Book Uncle looks different.

"Good morning, Yasmin-ma," he says.
He's not smiling.

The books are still in their boxes. He
hasn't even set them out yet, the way he
does each morning.

51

What's wrong?

Book Uncle is just standing there with a pink paper in his hand. He puts the paper in his pocket. He takes it out again, then puts it back once more. He shuffles his feet.

"What's wrong?" I ask. He is still not smiling. It jumbles me up.

"I can't do this anymore," he says.

I stare at him. What does he mean?

"They're telling me," he says, "that if I want to run my lending library here, I must get a permit."

A permit?

"Can't you get one?" I ask.

He shakes his head. "It costs too much. I can't afford it."

Then he says, "You want to give me back that book?"

He sounds so sad that I nearly burst into tears.

"I need to …" I hand it back to him.

I was going to say, *I need to get another book*. But before I can finish, Book Uncle takes the book from my hand. He puts it in a box. He picks up the box. He carries it over the broken pavement and stacks it on top of other boxes on his wooden cart. He does not even look at me.

He rolls the cart up the road — *ga-*

da-gadaa, goodoo-goodoo. He does not look back.

Over the wall that circles Horizon Apartment Flats, I meet the eyes of the istri lady. She moves her iron up and down her board. She shakes her head.

"What happened?" I wail.

"Someone wrote a letter to Mayor S. L. Yogaraja," says the istri lady. "It was a complaint. About our Book-ayya. Who would do a thing like that?"

The school bus is grinding its way towards my stop. I'd better go.

I don't want to get on that bus. I want to chase after Book Uncle. I want to say, "Wait! There must be some mistake!"

Instead I have to run to the bus stop.

There is so much I want to know. What was in that pink paper? Who would be so mean to Book Uncle? Why would anyone write a letter complaining about him? And where are all his patrons who come and go, giving and taking books, day after day after day?

Can't anyone help him?

I want to know all this, and there is no book that can tell me. What's more, for the first time in four hundred and two mornings, I don't have a new book to read.

11

Shocked

"WOULD YOU believe someone wrote a letter complaining about Book Uncle?" I say to Reeni on the bus.

She just stares at me with big round eyes. Then she looks away.

I try making jokes.

I try showing her the inside of my book bag where the lining was torn and I didn't know it, but when I followed a jingling noise, I found a bunch of change.

Nothing.

She won't talk to me in school, not even at our shared desk, not in maths or science,

Tamil or Hindi or English. Just won't talk.

When we get to school, Anil tries to juggle two pieces of chalk. He tries to make Reeni laugh, but she won't, won't, won't.

Mrs. Rao says, "Anil, sit down, or you'll have to go have a little chat with Indira Ma'am in the office."

All of which means yes, of course I said some things I shouldn't have. But it's not just me, is it? Anil was just trying to make things better. Can't Reeni see that?

What's wrong? I want to help but how can I do anything if she won't unbutton her lip and say one word?

When I'm ready to open up my tiffin box under the banyan tree at lunch break, I see Reeni sitting by herself. I can't stand it anymore.

"Would you like some dried mango?" I ask.

I am really trying to say, *Reeni, please*

talk to me because you're my friend, and I have to tell you all about Book Uncle and how can I do that if you won't talk to me? Aren't you my friend?

So I am shocked, completely shocked, when instead of saying, *Thank you, I'd like some dried mango*, or even, *Go away. I don't want your silly dried mango*, she bursts into tears.

12

Trapped by Words

I AM MORE than shocked, I am flabber-
gasted, which means stunned, staggered,
astonished.

When Reeni is done crying and her
eyes and nose have turned all red from it,
she tells me.

"My daddy's lost his job so he's going
to stay home now and Mummy's working
extra hours at the TV station."

"Lost his job?"

"That's what I just said," Reeni says.

I try to make sense of it. Arvind Uncle has lost his job? I know what that

means, of course, and it is not good. It is an odd way to say it, I think. It sounds as if you just misplaced the job. Woke up one morning not remembering where you left it or something.

When you lose a job, they ask you to leave and not come back. Like Book Uncle and his lending library.

"Mummy's getting headaches from working too hard," Reeni says. "And to make things worse, she used to do the bookkeeping for the Horizon Apartment Flats Association and Daddy says he'll do that now to help out."

"So that's good," I say. "Isn't it?"

"No!" wails Reeni. "It's horrible. They fight all the time about invoices and bills, and why the maintenance company got overpaid three years ago."

Oh. That sounds bad.

"And when I try to stop them," Reeni says, "They say, 'Go to your room.' 'Stay out of this, Reeni,' they say. 'You won't understand,' they say."

Reeni's words trap me in their net so I am speechless. Now I know why I hurt her when I wouldn't talk to her on the bus. When I said — oh, how I wish I could take back the thing I said and grind it into little pieces and throw it away.

Don't you know anything?

How could I say that to my best friend?

13

No Book

I MANAGE TO get through most of the school day, until the afternoon.

Mrs. Rao says, "Take out your books for silent reading time."

And I am frozen. Around me, everyone is getting books. From book bags. Desks. From piles behind Mrs. Rao's desk. From the bookshelf in the back of the class.

I cannot move. I want to run and get something to read, too. But I can't.

"You don't have a book, Yasmin?" asks Mrs. Rao.

"No," I mumble.

"Get one from the shelf," she says. "Come on, hurry. I know what an enthusiastic reader you are."

I try to pick a book off the classroom bookshelf.

I can't. I stare at the spines of books marching along the shelf. They blur into a stream of colors and letters.

I can't pick one. I can't choose. This has never happened to me before.

"Yasmin," says Mrs. Rao.

I'm the one who tells others about books I've read. Wapa calls me the world's biggest book fan. I'm the one who reads one book a day and will do so forever.

What is stopping me now?

I stick out my hand and grab a book off the shelf, any book. I go back to my desk. I open the book. The words float together, and I cannot read.

Someone has to do something about this bad news crashing on us all at once.

Reeni's father's job, Book Uncle's pink paper. Someone has to do something.

14

Riddles

THE AFTERNOON goes by, and I am getting more and more confused.

When I get home, I try not to look at the corner of St. Mary's Road and 1st Cross Street because I know how empty it will be. I do look and it is worse, much worse than I imagined.

No Book Uncle. No books. It makes my heart hurt.

I do my homework. Then I walk around the house. I try to read the karate book but the words swim before my eyes. There will be no new book tomorrow and the next day and the day after that.

My dream of one book a day has gone down the drain.

"Yasmin, come and have dinner," says Umma. "Chicken biryani with lime pickle."

I love biryani. But today not even chicken biryani with lime pickle will help.

I circle the dining table, circle it again. I can't make myself sit down.

"Yasmin," Wapa says. "Why are you prowling around like a tiger in a cage?"

I fall into my chair and it all comes spilling out. I tell them about Reeni's father losing his job and her parents fighting and how bad I feel about being mean to Reeni and what can I possibly do now?

They look at each other.

"Oh, dear," Umma says.

Oh, dear? Is that all? Sometimes

grown-ups can be very disappointing.

Wapa makes a cocoon with his hands. He rests his chin on top of it and looks at his biryani.

"As the Pir says ..." he begins.

Ever since he did some research and discovered that we are distantly related to an eighteenth-century Tamil Sufi saint — very distantly, Umma says — Wapa deals with all challenges, big and small, by trying to channel Pir Baba.

I groan.

"Yasmin," Umma warns. She turns to my father as if she really wants to know what the Pir says.

Wapa puts on his best Pir-talking look.

"Pir Baba says, 'A loving disposition towards one's neighbor lightens the heart as wings.' How about that, my Minu?"

I give up. Why do grown-ups always speak in riddles?

"Go to sleep early today," Umma says,

"because you-know-who will be here at the break of day."

"Nadira," Wapa says to Umma, but he's looking at me.

"What?" says Umma. "You think Yasmin doesn't know that your big brother is a bully and a petty tyrant and wants us all to go live in the village and doesn't like the fact that I have a college degree?"

Wapa sighs and rubs his forehead. I can see he already has a headache coming on.

I go to sleep that night and dream of the doves in Book Uncle's book. Caught in a net, the doves all fly up in the air together. They carry the net with them.

And the hunter? Well, he runs on the ground as fast as he can, but he can't catch up with them. So after a while he stops trying.

In the end the doves find a safe place to land. They ask a friendly mole to chew through the net so they can wriggle free.

I wake up and find that my teeth are chewing away on nothing. This is not a good feeling, because what is the use of busy teeth when your mouth is empty?

15

Not Bad?

THUD! THUMP! *Crash!*

That is more than the day breaking. It is Rafiq Uncle. I run out of my room to see what's going on. Rafiq Uncle's baggage, it seems, got dropped on the floor. That's why he is now yelling at the istri lady's son, Selvaraj.

"What do you think, this is a sack of onions? That suitcase costs money, my boy. Money!"

Selvaraj is straightening up the suitcase and trying to dust it off. He is trying to say it was a mistake and he is sorry, but no one can get a word in, once Rafiq Uncle gets going.

"Oh, Yasmin, is it?" Rafiq Uncle says, turning his attention to me.

Selvaraj makes a quick getaway, grabbing the rupee notes that Umma slips him to make up for my uncle's rudeness.

Wapa takes his big brother's bags into the extra bedroom. Umma puts out breakfast. I get a lecture on the evils of living in the big city.

Umma has made puttu for breakfast, which I love-love-love for its grated coconut and soft steamed morsels of rice that melt in your mouth.

We eat for a while in grateful silence. Even Rafiq Uncle is silenced by the dreaminess of that puttu. Soon the big plate is down to one last piece. Rafiq Uncle and I both stretch out our hands at the same time.

I meet his eyes. He opens his mouth.

"You have it, Uncle," I say quickly. "I have to go to school."

He snaps his lips shut, as if he is disappointed that he can't scold me for being greedy.

As I put my plate in the sink and wash my hands, I hear him saying, through his last mouthful of puttu, "Not bad, Nadira. Not bad at all."

Not bad? My Umma makes the best puttu in the whole world. Now I wish I had grabbed that last piece. Rafiq Uncle doesn't deserve it.

16

Ten Whole Words

I AM HURRYING down the stairs, happy to be away from my bad-tempered uncle. I'm almost all the way to the ground floor when I hear someone huffing and puffing up the stairwell.

It is Chinna Abdul Sahib of 2B. He's carrying a big box. He's breathing heavily. He's rounding the corner and now we are face to face.

Oh, no! The box slips.

I grab at it double-quick so it doesn't fall. It is heavy. I brace myself so I can hold it up. It would be terrible if I let it fall.

From his face, I am sure it contains something very precious. Possibly a drum.

Chinna Abdul Sahib nods twice. I take that to mean, *Thank you, and will you help me carry this box?* Funny how I know exactly what he means even when he says nothing, while my uncle uses a hundred words and I can't find much meaning in anything he says.

I hold one end of the box with my two hands. Chinna Abdul Sahib holds the other end. I walk up the stairs backwards, and he comes up after me. Step by step by step.

There. We put the box down carefully outside 2B.

Then Chinna Abdul Sahib pulls out a bunch of jingly keys and opens his door. I help him lift the box over the threshold and place it on the floor.

"Is that one of your drums?" I ask.

He scratches his beard. He stares at the wall.

Then, "You want to see?" he says.

You could knock me down with a feather, which means that I'm very surprised. In all the time that I have seen Chinna Abdul Sahib coming and going, I don't think I have ever heard him speak a single word.

He opens up the box. I take a peek.

I was right. It is a drum. A giant pot-drum.

"What's that?" I point to the shiny flecks showing through the clay.

"Brass," he says, "for a ringing sound."

They make this clay pot with bits of brass? This is one thing I have never come across in a book.

He knocks on the pot with his knuckle. It rings. It sings. It has a voice all its own. I can see why Chinna Abdul Sahib does not need to say much. His ghatam does all the talking.

A clock strikes from somewhere inside the flat. Eight o'clock!

"I have to go," I say.

I don't want to miss my bus.

"Very kind of you," he calls after me, "to help me with my drum."

That is ten whole words he's used up just for me.

17

Number Problems

AFTER SCHOOL, Anil gets off the bus with me at Horizon Apartment Flats. His mother has a meeting, so she can't be home when he gets back from school. His aunty, who lives with them, has gone out of town for a few days.

Anil does not think he needs a grown-up around to keep an eye on him, but his mother disagrees. So here he is, coming home with me where Umma is in charge.

"I have an idea," I tell Anil.

"What?"

I am all ready to throw our bags down and get a snack and then head out of the flat to carry out my great idea, which is all about being someone and doing something.

Umma insists, homework first. We get to work. We have no choice. Soon there is no sound from us but rustling pages and scratching pencils.

We finish our history homework.

Then Hindi. We finish reading our Hindi pages and then we have to answer questions about them. I decide that I like Hindi, with its lines on top so the letters hang down like rows of election campaign flags. My lines and strokes don't always come out even, but I like doing them anyway.

Anil is wriggly, but soon he says he's done, too.

That leaves a page of number problems between us and my plan. Ready? We work on these together. There is no sign between the numbers:

+ - x ÷. We have to fill them in.

"Go," says Anil.

50 ? 32=18

"Minus," I say. "Anil, your turn."

88 ? 22=110

"Times?" Anil says.

"No, pay attention!"

"I am paying attention." He looks again. "Oh, plus."

Back and forth we go. Anil gets a few wrong and then a few more. Sometimes he seems to make wild guesses. Maybe he's just fed up. I know the feeling.

Then, hurray! We get to the end of the number problems.

"Want to go downstairs?" I say.

"Hiya!" says Anil, leaping up in joy.

We tell Umma we're going out.

"Come back before it gets dark," she says.

"Okay, Umma," I say.

"Okay, Aunty," Anil says.

Umma hugs us both at the door, which makes Anil do a quick block-punch.

"Be careful, Warrior Anil!" says Umma, and he grins.

Anil wants to know what we are going to do.

"Wait," I tell him. "Just wait."

"Are you going to call Reeni?" he says.

I nod. "Yes. That's part of the plan."

18

A Delegation

We stop at 3B. We invite Reeni along. And she says, yes, yes, she'll come and we are three again. Reeni has brought us sticky tamarind sweets. We pucker our lips over their mouthwatering sourness.

Our flip-floppy chappals *slip-slap-slap* down the stairs and into the compound, under the coconut palm and the frangipani tree that drops its pink and white flowers on top of the istri lady's booth.

"What's chasing you chickens?" she demands.

"Do you know where Book Uncle lives?" I ask.

She throws her head back and laughs out loud before whirling around to spit a stream of betel and tobacco juice at the ground behind her. She turns back to us with a red-toothed grin.

Wapa says that stuff can kill you. I don't see the istri lady ready to fall over yet.

"I know where everyone lives," she says. Then she bellows, "Selvaraj!"

Her son runs back from the corner tea shop where he's been chatting with the autorickshaw drivers. He rushes to a smart stop, like a soldier reporting to his commanding officer.

Selvaraj takes over the ironing booth, and the istri lady marches us down the road and left at the petrol bunk. Past Celebration Sweets and the La-la-la Restaurant. Past the Mercury Medicals lab and pharmacy, three doctors' offices, a dentist and a phone repair shop which is also a phone-fax-Internet-copy place. All the way past blocks and blocks of houses and apartments we go, to a tiny little house that has almost disappeared under the leaning-down branches of a giant mango tree.

I knock on the door. We wait. Shuffling noises sound from inside the tiny house.

Then, "My goodness me."

Book Uncle opens the door. His eyes blink at us from behind his fat glasses.

"A delegation. What a surprise. Come in, come in."

The house is so small that when the istri lady and Reeni and Anil and I step inside, we fill it up. There is only enough room for Book Uncle, the four of us, and the shelves and shelves of books.

What a lot of books! Hundreds and hundreds of them. Boxes of books are stacked on the floor, with just enough room for a person to walk around and between them.

The book smell in the air turns me dizzy with joy.

When I grow up I will line all the walls of my house with books, just like this.

19

Notice

IN HIS TINY house, over tiny glasses of tea, Book Uncle tells us how he got started with his books. He began collecting them when he was a young teacher in a village near the city, where the school was too poor to have any books.

"Once I started, I couldn't stop," he says. "My wife and I, we both collected books."

"Was she a teacher, too?" I ask.

"She was." His eyes go to a picture on a bookshelf. It is a picture of a lady with a gentle face. She is wearing a shiny-bordered sari. She has flowers in her hair.

"Is that her?" Reeni says.

Book Uncle nods.

"She was a good soul," the istri lady murmurs. "Kind and generous she was." She narrows her eyes at us, so we can see that there is a sad story in that picture, and we know not to say anything more.

When he retired from teaching, Book Uncle decided to set up his free lending library, where you don't have to sign up and get a card or pay a fee, where even if you have no place to sleep, if you can read a little bit, there will be a book for you.

"And not only that," the istri lady says. "You taught people how to read. You helped me open up a bank account so I could save some money, and you taught me how to write my name. You do kind things for so many people."

That is the longest I have ever heard the istri lady speak without yelling at someone.

Book Uncle says, "People ask me, 'Why don't you charge for the books you lend?' But you see ..." He waves a hand around him. "What do I need money for? I have my little pension which comes promptly every month, and the landlady is kind enough not to raise my rent."

"Only now they're not going to let you give your books away?" the istri lady says.

"Alas," says Book Uncle. "The city has given me notice."

Notice. It is a word that makes you sit up and pay attention. That pink paper was the notice.

It said that Book Uncle does not have a permit for a commercial establishment.

Therefore his lending library is an illegal operation and must be shut down.

If he wants to stay open, he has to pay a lot of money to the city.

I look around me now. I notice that the curtains are faded. The furniture is old. Book Uncle must not have a lot of money.

"That is not fair!" Reeni says. "You should complain."

"To the mayor," Anil says.

Book Uncle shakes his head. "The notice was from the mayor's office," he says. "Maybe it's part of a city project. Catching up with uncollected fees or something like that. What can I do?"

I open my mouth. Because I know it's not part of any city project. They sent him that notice because someone wrote a letter of complaint. But I catch the istri lady's eye. It holds a warning glint. I say nothing.

Book Uncle sees us off at the door. He thanks us. I don't know for what. We haven't done anything.

As we walk home, I say, "I'm confused. Why did the city send that notice?"

The istri lady says, "It was that letter, of course."

"What letter?" says Reeni.

I explain.

"What a mean person," Reeni says, "to complain about Book Uncle."

"Mean and nasty," Anil agrees.

"I didn't tell him about it," says the istri lady. "What is the use? It would only hurt his feelings."

20

A-One Candidate

I WAKE UP LATE the next morning and barely make it out of the door in time to catch the bus. Good thing the driver is in a singing mood. He does not yell at me.

Reeni and Anil and I talk about Book Uncle.

"I can't believe that Mayor S.L. Yogaraja would want to shut him down!" I say.

"I wonder who wrote that horrible letter?" Reeni says.

"Karate Samuel would be a better mayor," Anil says. "He wouldn't shut Book Uncle down."

"My wapa says anyone would be better than Mayor SLY," I say.

Anil does a quick-twisting block with both hands. It's his karate way to say *Definitely*.

I try to twist my hands like that but I can't. My hands don't work like Anil's. But maybe trying to twist them jiggled my brain, because right at that moment I realize something.

That notice, the pink notice, is plain flat-out wrong. They can't make Book Uncle pay a fee. Commercial. Commercial is when you sell something. Book Uncle's not selling anything.

The bus turns into school and stops.

I explain my big realization as we inch forward in line to get off the jam-packed bus.

"You're right," Reeni says. "He's not selling anything."

"Yes, but does the mayor understand that?" Anil says.

"Maybe not," I say.

"Who said mayor?" says the bus driver.

"I did," says Anil.

"Be happy, friends!" the driver tells us. "Soon we'll have a new mayor! His Excellency the Most Honorable A-One Mayor-ayya, Karaaaaaate Samuel!"

He stops and looks a little embarrassed. We've caught him being a live campaign commercial. Now he clears his throat and goes back to being a serious bus driver.

"Are you going to vote for him?" I ask.

"*Am* I going to vote for him?" says the bus driver. "Am I going to *vote* for him? Am *I* going to — "

"Okay, I get it," I say.

He says, "Naturally I'm going to vote for him."

And that is what gives me my next big idea.

21

Hundreds of Letters

IF ONE COMPLAINING letter can cause a problem, maybe hundreds of letters can fix it. The doves were trapped, but when they flapped their wings together, they could lift up the net and fly it far away from the hunter — first things first — and then get help from a friendly mole who cut them free.

You may not think those things follow one another necessarily, but they can and they do in that story.

It's complicated, yes. I'm finding out that real life can also be that way.

I tell Mrs. Rao about Book Uncle's notice.

"Mrs. Rao, ma'am," I say. "We should write letters. We should write them to all the people who are running for mayor. And we should send the letters before the election."

Mrs. Rao listens.

"A most interesting idea," she says. "Tell me more."

I tell her because I have thought it all over.

"We should make a list of all the candidates. Everyone can pick who they want to write to."

"Wonderful," says Mrs. Rao. "I'll bring last Sunday's paper with all the political party addresses on the center page."

"I've written my letter already," I say. "Can I read it?"

"You can and you may," says Mrs. Rao.

Dear Karate Samuel Sir,

I want to tell you about a special person in our city. We call him Book Uncle. He has a lending library on the corner of St. Mary's Road and 1st Cross Street. He has books for everyone. He loves his books like friends.

The city is making Book Uncle get a permit. Why? He does not sell anything. He simply lends his books out to anyone who wants to borrow one. If you take a book and keep it, that is fine with him also.

If you get elected will you help Book Uncle?

Sincerely,

Yasmin Z. Kader

I finish reading. The classroom falls dead silent. My throat is so dry I think it's going to close up. Then everyone claps-claps-claps.

"Who else is going to write a letter about Book Uncle?" asks Mrs. Rao.

A few hands go up. Then a few more. Before too long, many, many kids in the class are volunteering to write their letters about Book Uncle.

Book Uncle is quickly becoming our election issue.

At recess time Reeni and Anil and I tell everyone we know about the letters that we are collecting. They all tell their friends who tell their friends. It turns out that some of those friends or friends of friends are also Book Uncle's patrons.

Of course they are. I am not the only one who borrows books from him. I know that.

Still, it makes me happy to see my good idea become a real election issue.

The message spreads like wildfire. That is to say, fast.

Soon Mrs. Rao's desk is covered with letters. Some are for Mayor SLY. Some are for those other people who want to be mayor. But most of the letters — a wild and fiery number of them — are addressed to Karate Samuel.

22

Connections

THE NEXT TUESDAY is Republic Day. They show us the big parade on TV, broadcast all the way from Delhi. Even Rafiq Uncle is impressed, I can see. He can't find anything to criticize.

The President of India gives her talk. Floats from all the states go past. Dancers dance and the marching bands play-play-play.

After that, the local news comes on. First a few headlines. National news. Then local. After that, we cut to a studio where all the candidates for mayor wait, ready to be interviewed!

There's Mayor SLY with his pointy mustache. And one man with a bald head, one wearing a dazzling white shirt. A lady in a printed sari. And Karate Samuel, looking very fine with a rose in his buttonhole.

All these people want to be mayor.

The interviewer opens with some welcoming remarks. Then the talk begins. Back and forth, back and forth.

I wait for someone to say something about Book Uncle.

No one does. No one.

What is wrong with them? I try not to fidget and still no one says anything, which makes me so angry I cannot sit still, which makes Rafiq Uncle demand in an irritated voice, "What is the matter, Yasmin?"

"Book Uncle!" I burst out. "He's an important election issue."

He looks completely baffled so I explain

it as well as I can. I tell him the whole story, all the way from how I mean to read a book every day for the rest of my life. The pink notice. Mrs. Rao. My letter-writing campaign. Everything.

"We wrote all those letters," I say. "And still no one cares."

It does not look as if Rafiq Uncle is paying any attention to my explanation. Instead he glares at my father.

"Who is this Book Uncle?" Rafiq Uncle demands to know.

Umma takes a deep breath. She picks up a small brass bell that sits on the end table next to the sofa.

"Thambi," says Rafiq Uncle to Wapa. "What do you have to say about your daughter roaming about here and there all by herself, reading who-knows-what trash from the street corner?"

Umma lets out that deep breath she took a moment ago. She looks as if she would like to throw the bell at Rafiq Uncle.

My father comes to life. My father sits up straight. He clears his throat.

"Rafiq-anna," he says in his most respectful tone to his big brother. "I trust my daughter. I trust her judgment. I will not look over her shoulder as if I suspect that she is up to no good."

Umma's head jerks up. She puts the bell down. Then she covers her mouth with her hand.

Is she smiling? I can't tell.

Rafiq Uncle says, "Of course you trust her. I'm not saying — "

Which is when I interrupt, not to be rude or anything, but because I can't stand it anymore.

"Please. Rafiq Uncle. Don't talk about me as if I'm not here!"

And that silences them all. Totally.

I say, "Umma, Wapa, I'm going to see Reeni. Is that okay?"

My parents nod.

I run out of the door and across the landing and knock on Reeni's door.

"We have to do something to help Book Uncle," I tell her. "It's up to us."

"What can we do?" Reeni says.

Somehow my confusion has been swept away by hearing Wapa talk back to his big brother for the first time ever. I don't know why, but I now see things very, very clearly.

"Reeni," I say. "There just weren't enough doves lifting that net. We have to get more."

Reeni is a little confused about what doves have to do with a piece of paper and the city.

But after I clear that one up, she says, "Oh, now I get it. Of course I'll help you."

We go door to door, up and down Horizon Apartment Flats. We tell everyone about Book Uncle.

"Whoever you vote for," we say, "that

person has to let Book Uncle keep his street-corner lending library. Don't you agree?"

Chinna Abdul Sahib nods. "I know him well," he says.

"You do?" How does he know Book Uncle? He never speaks two words to anyone.

Here I am getting that surprise feather feeling again. Chinna Abdul Sahib drums against the doorframe.

He says, "Music books. He gave me music books years ago, when I thought I wanted to be an accountant. He changed my life."

He's one of Book Uncle's patrons! I have never heard Chinna Abdul Sahib make such a long speech.

"That Book-ayya is a good man," says the istri lady from behind the tall-growing-taller pile of clothes she is collecting from the boy in 2C and the lady in 2A.

She counts the clothes carefully — four rupees each for the pants and the saris, two for the shirts and blouses.

"That will be twenty-six for you and forty-two for you," she says. I'm sure she's right. She did that in her head. I would need paper and pencil.

I wonder if Book Uncle taught the istri lady how to add.

"I don't know him," says the lady in 2A, who is new to the building. I tell her all about how Book Uncle always has the right book for the right person on the right day.

"I'll give my vote to whoever promises to help him," says the istri lady. The lady in 2A nods-nods-nods. She is on our side.

"I miss him," says the boy from 2C. "I'll tell my parents and my grandmother." So he's a patron, too.

"We have to save Book Uncle's place,"

we say to Reeni's mother in 3B. We tell her why.

"No question," says Shoba Aunty, between taking sips of coffee from the mug in one hand and sending a text message on her phone with the other. Shoba Aunty is always doing more than one thing, which is probably why she is looking a little tired.

"You must make it a media issue," she tells us. "Take it to TV."

Reeni looks at me. I look at her.

"How?" we say together.

Shoba Aunty says, "Connections, my dear girls. It's who you know."

My heart sinks. "I don't ..."

"Yes, you do," Reeni says. "Mummy!"

Shoba Aunty nods. "I'll put in a word at the TV station. You watch the news. What's today? Tuesday? How about Thursday evening, okay?"

23

Fine

BY THURSDAY, RAFIQ Uncle has gone back to the village. He has finished his business in the city.

That evening, Reeni comes over to 3A to watch the news. She arrives early, so we go out to the balcony.

"Umma," I say before I close the door behind us. "Don't forget to tell us when the news starts."

"I don't think I have ever seen you so eager to watch the news," my mother grumbles, but there is a gleam in her eye. She's been gleamy since my uncle left.

And another funny thing. I think my parents have forgotten to scold me for being rude to Rafiq Uncle.

Reeni and I stand on the balcony and look at the parrots fussing in the raintree. The pink-flowery, feather-leafy branches have to be clipped every now and then, so the squirrels don't get into the flats and make a big mess.

Reeni coughs and shuffles her feet.

"Are you sick?" I ask. "Have you caught a cold? Does your stomach hurt?"

She looks as if she would like to curl up in some corner and disappear quietly.

"No," she says. "I'm not sick."

"Then what?"

"Nothing," she says.

"Something," I insist.

"Nothing."

"Something. Tell me."

"I can't."

"Am I your friend?" I demand.

"Ye-e-s," she says.

"Then? So? Tell!"

"Okay, fine." She tells. "It's Daddy."

"Your daddy?" I lower my voice. "Are your parents still fighting?"

She shakes her head so hard her plaits flop from side to side.

"No," she says. "But that's how I found out, because they're talking to each other again and I overheard them. They were arguing about Book Uncle all this time! And I didn't even know."

"What? What did they say?" Why is it so hard to get this story out of my friend? I try to be patient. "Reeni, just tell me from the beginning, okay?"

She says all in a rush, "He sent the letter. He did. But it was for the association, because otherwise we would have to pay a fine. He was only trying to help, Yasmin."

"What letter? What fine? Reeni, I'm

not a mind reader. Will you tell me what you're talking about?"

"The letter to the city!" she wails. "Complaining about Book Uncle! Only he wasn't complaining, really. Just explaining that it was Book Uncle and not us."

What does she mean? That must be the letter that the istri lady told us about, that some nasty person sent to the city saying nasty things about Book Uncle.

The nasty person was Reeni's dad?

And what does she mean, we would have to pay a fine? That does not seem fine at all. It all seems more puzzling than ever.

"Yasmin," Umma calls. "The news is going to start in just a minute."

24

The News

FORTUNATELY, THERE is no time for Reeni to stay upset.

She quickly tells me everything on the way inside from the balcony to the sofa, where we settle down to watch the TV news. The city was trying to fine us. Us! All the people in Horizon Apartment Flats. They were going to do this because they thought we had set up the lending library just outside our building compound. They called the library clutter.

Well, that was two things they got wrong! Reeni's daddy tried to tell them the library belonged to Book Uncle and not us. He tried to explain that it was not clutter.

"He didn't say nasty things about Book Uncle," Reeni says. "You know he would never do that."

Why would the city even care about Book Uncle's lending library being outside our building? We didn't mind, so why should anyone else? What is wrong with all these people?

"Don't worry," I whisper to Reeni. "We'll do something."

She looks as if she wants to believe me but she's not sure if she does. Truthfully, I don't know if *I* believe me.

There they are in a row, all the candidates. They begin with things I don't know much about, like what do they feel about the new Techno-Zone, and do they have a drinking water plan for the city? I should try to remember those things, in case I ever need to know about them.

Then the TV person says, "I understand you have all received letters about a certain gentleman in our city ..."

"Mmm," says Mayor S. L. Yogaraja, looking unhappy.

"... who runs a street-corner library," says the TV person.

"Y-y-yes," says another candidate.

"Something like that," says a third.

"I wish to clarify," Mayor SLY says, his hands making designs in the air. "This so-called Book Uncle person ... he is, you know, not to put too fine a point on it, breaking the law. I have received complaints. We must make our city clean and green. Clean and green, yes. That's my motto."

The TV person coughs. He turns to Karate Samuel. "And you, sir? Do you have anything to say on this matter?'"

"Yes, in*deed*," says Karate Samuel, all bright and ready. "I have received many,

many letters, even from children. About one Mr. Book Uncle."

At last, at last, at long long last! I am so excited I jump up and down. My parents look at each other and they smile in that way grown-ups have when they're trying to understand kids, but really, it is too much for them so it's best to smile and carry on.

Karate Samuel is carrying on. "I understand Mr. Book Uncle makes it possible for children to get good books. Can you think of a better thing to do?"

The TV person says no, he can't.

"He is a symbol of our city's pride in elderly people, children and literacy."

Karate Samuel pauses here, as if he now expects applause.

He has said some nice things about Book Uncle. That is a start. Slowly, I begin to clap my hands. Reeni sniffles, but she claps her hands, too. All at once our little flat fills with the sound of people clapping their hands.

I turn to see. Who else is here?

Why, the room is full. While we have been watching the news, it seems all the people who live in Horizon Apartment Flats have come to watch it with us. Even the newly-marrieds from 1B are looking at the TV instead of at each other.

"See?" I say to Reeni. "If one letter can cause a problem, many letters can make it right."

She nods. But she still looks as if she's taken a step, expecting to find pavement under her feet, but it isn't there.

25

Just One Minute

THE NEXT DAY Wapa comes home from work a little early. He offers to take me to the La-la-la Restaurant for mango ice cream.

"Yay! Ice cream? Can I call Reeni?"

"Of course."

I ring Reeni's doorbell. She asks Arvind Uncle. He goes and gets his wallet. Which is how not two, not three, but four of us end up around a table at the La-la-la Restaurant, chatting over little bowls of creamy melt-in-your-mouth mango ice cream.

Ice cream is not the only thing to share. There is news as well. Reeni's daddy has a job! He is going to be working at the TV station. They needed an accountant and now they have hired him. He is excited, so Reeni is excited, too. And so am I, since that is how friendship works.

"Samples of new surprise ice cream for anyone?" the waiter says.

Reeni and I both want to try the new surprise ice cream. The waiter says he'll be back in just one minute.

As he disappears into the back of the La-la-la Restaurant, the talk at our table turns to Book Uncle.

"Would you believe the mistake I made?" Arvind Uncle says. He talks about that letter he wrote to Mayor SLY. "Bad mistake, I tell you. I was upset because our association got threatened with a fine of two thousand rupees for debris and clutter on the pavement."

"Why?" Wapa asks. "Why would they suddenly decide to fine us?"

"Politics and crookedness, that's why," says Reeni's father. He said that after he sent his explaining-not-complaining letter, he got suspicious. So he asked a few questions. He found out that a crew of city workers had been sent to clean up the street just outside the Palm Tree Hotel.

The Palm Tree Hotel is down the road from Horizon Apartment Flats. Why was the city suddenly so worried about the road outside the hotel? So Reeni's daddy found out who owns that hotel.

"It seems the owner's daughter is getting married and the future in-laws are coming here from Mumbai for the wedding."

Naturally they're going to stay in that very fancy hotel that we walk past all the time but have never been in. They want to get the sidewalks cleared and cleaned in time for the wedding.

We know that Palm Tree Hotel very well. Whenever the pressure in our water taps goes down, Umma grumbles, *Look at the lawn of that Palm Tree Hotel! Look at those fountains. They're drinking up our water.*

The just-one-minute waiter finally brings little sample cups with very pink scoops in them. Pomegranate. It tastes zippy and sweet.

"So who is he?" says Wapa. "The owner of the Palm Tree Hotel?"

Arvind Uncle lowers his voice. "You won't believe it. One of the reporters at the station told Shoba. It's the mayor."

"The mayor?"

Suddenly an ice cream scooper has scooped a giant hole in my insides. "Mayor SLY?"

What? This is why he wants Book Uncle off the pavement at the corner of St. Mary's Road and 1st Cross Street? To clean up the street for his daughter's wedding?

"All the hoopla about fines and permits is just an excuse," says Arvind Uncle.

It's unbelievable.

Book Uncle is not debris. He is not clutter. How can anyone say that about a lending library that puts the right book into the right hands on the right day?

That sweet and zippy pomegranate ice cream suddenly tastes flat.

26

One at a Time

"Want to buy some papaya?" Late that evening, the fruit man brings a bagful across the road. "Sweet and nice, guaranteed."

"Not right now," I say, "but wait till you hear this." And I tell him about Mayor SLY and the wedding and the guests who will be staying at the Palm Tree Hotel.

The fruit man listens carefully. He wiggles and waggles his head to show me that he gets it.

"See that cart?" He points across the road. The fruit on his cart is arranged in perfect pyramids — guavas, sapotas, oranges, papayas. Each pyramid has many at the bottom, many more in between and one on the very, very top.

"How do you think you make a pile like that?" he demands.

"Carefully?" says Reeni.

The fruit man laughs. "One at a time," he says. "One at a time. It's the only way. Come on. Get busy. Start piling up your fruit."

"What do you mean?" I ask. "What fruit?" He's speaking in riddles now, just like my parents.

"I mean you need people on your side," he says. "So you must tell as many people as you can. We don't have much time left."

He may be a riddle-talker, but the fruit man is right.

I get busy. I talk to Anil and Reeni. The people we know are kids, so that is who we tell. All day long in school, we tell-tell-

tell. We tell our friends and classmates to tell their parents and their aunties and uncles and grandparents and friends and the people next door. Tell them that the only reason the mayor wants Book Uncle off the pavement is to clean up the road for his daughter's wedding.

How fair is that? Does the mayor think he owns every street corner? Is Book Uncle no more than debris? Clutter? Tell-tell-tell, we urge them. Keep up the telling.

In the next two days, we set out again and again, up and down St. Mary's Road.

"Don't vote for Mayor SLY," we tell people. "Vote for Karate Samuel. He cares about Book Uncle. Didn't he say so on TV?"

By Sunday evening when the parrots have settled down to sleep in the raintree branches, we drag ourselves back to Horizon Apartment Flats. My feet hurt. Reeni has a blister on her heel. But we are wearing big smiles, because we have done good work and maybe, just maybe, Mayor SLY will lose this election, and Book Uncle will be back on the pavement with his books.

27

Counting Chickens

WEDNESDAY IS ELECTION day. Umma votes. Wapa votes. They come back with little ink marks on their fingers to show that they have voted.

Reeni and I go up and down the stairs asking everyone in Horizon Apartment Flats.

"Have you voted yet?" "Have you?" "Have you?"

The newly-marrieds have voted.

"Yes, yes," they tell us together, holding up their index fingers with the little inky marks for proof.

Shoba Aunty has voted. Arvind Uncle has voted, too. Reeni made sure of that. Chinna Abdul Sahib has voted.

Has Book Uncle voted? We race around the corner and all the way to his little house.

"Have you voted?" we ask him.

"What's the use?" he says.

"Book Uncle!" I cry. "You have to vote."

With Reeni's help I tell Book Uncle all the things we have been doing to get his library back to its corner.

"If Karate Samuel wins, he'll let you put your library back. Don't you think you should vote for him?"

He looks at me through his thick round glasses.

"We mustn't count our chickens before they are hatched."

"What chickens?" Reeni and I say together. Then I get it. These chickens are like marbles and bricks and flapping doves.

126

"Book Uncle," I say, "forget the chickens. If you vote you will be one of those doves that managed to escape from the hunter."

He stares at me.

"The doves," I remind him. "In that book that you lent me."

"You are right," he says slowly, in a thinking-very-hard kind of voice. "I'll go now. Is there still time?"

"Yes," we say. "There is still a little time before the polls close."

We see him on his way. Then we head back, feeling as if we have done a full day's work. Reeni goes home. I go back to 3A, where Wapa is boiling rice.

"Where's Umma?" I ask. He tells me she's taken the phone to the shop to be repaired.

"It's lost its ring tone," Wapa says. "But Nathan's Electronics said they could fix it."

"Oh!" I cry. "We should have gone to

the shops! We talked to lots of people but we didn't talk to the shopkeepers."

The rice water boils over. Wapa says something under his breath, then turns it quickly into a cough.

"Talk to them about what?" says Wapa.

"About Book Uncle." I explain about the fruit man's pyramids of guavas, sapotas, oranges and papayas, and getting big things done little by little and gathering the people we need. I tell him how I have been talking to people all day long, urging them to vote for Karate Samuel because he'll help Book Uncle and Mayor SLY won't.

Wapa turns away from the steaming rice. He leans against the kitchen counter and looks at me. He looks and looks. He looks at me as if I have suddenly grown wings and am about to begin flapping around the room.

I cannot tell if Wapa is smiling or serious. Is it possible to be both?

"Yasmin," he says at last. "Election day is almost over. We'll know the results in a few more days. There's nothing else you can do."

He is right. But still I go to my room and count the books on my shelf as if they've hatched into chickens.

28

Whose Victory Is It, Anyway?

IT TAKES TOO many days for the election results to come out on TV. I think I will go crazy from all the waiting. Why can't they add up the votes sooner, now that everything is supposed to be double-quick with the Internet and all? Why are they so slow? People are always telling kids to hurry up. Now it seems as if the grown-up world has slowed to a crawl.

A whole week goes by the way snails are supposed to. Although really, I have never seen a snail. They don't just wander around in the city. I get grumpy thinking of all the things I have not seen and do not know. Including, now, those election results.

On Wednesday, at dinner time, I pull the clothes off the washing line. I wash my hands and put the plates out for dinner. Then I help Umma to put out rice and egg curry and crunchy fried yams and grated carrots with mustard seeds on top.

By the time we finish eating, it is dark. The breezes blow in from the faraway beach over the city rooftops.

Reeni comes over. I go up to the terrace with her and pick up the flowers that have blown off the raintree. Their puffy pink petals are turning limp. We roll them between our fingers and let the pollen streak our hands.

"Reeni! Yasmin!" Shoba Aunty is calling up from their balcony. "Come down. Come listen."

We hurry down, startling the lizards

that are busy eating insects around the terrace lights.

On TV they are announcing the election results.

"Oh, look, look, look!" Reeni shrieks and points.

By a margin of 3,879 votes — that is a lot of votes, isn't it? — KARATE SAMUEL HAS WON! It's all over the TV news and the radio news. Within minutes, it's also all over the people-shouting-to-each-other news.

We run up the stairs telling everyone. We run down the stairs telling everyone all over again in case they didn't hear it the first time.

"He won!" we tell Chinna Abdul Sahib.

"Perfect," he says.

"He won!" we tell Shoba Aunty.

"We did it," she says. Arvind Uncle beams. They are not fighting anymore, it's clear.

"He won," we tell the newly-marrieds. They gaze happily at each other.

"He won," we tell the istri lady, who is closing up shop for the day.

"Yes," says the istri lady, closing the wooden doors of her ironing booth and clicking the lock. "But will he remember our Book-ayya?"

Her words sting. I want him to remember. I want it so badly that my stomach hurts.

What was the use of all that work? What if this Karate Samuel actor person who is now mayor forgets all about the one thing that everyone wants him to do? The one person we all want him to help?

Is the istri lady right? Will Mayor Karate Samuel forget about Book Uncle? Her stinging words buzz around in my mind like angry bees.

"You worry too much," says Reeni.

"I know," I say sadly. "I can't help it."

I go back to 3A. The TV is off and my parents are quiet. Everything feels empty because everything is over. I go to my room and I look at all the books on my shelf. And I think, *What can I do now?*

I pick up a book. It is the karate book that Book Uncle gave me. I should give it to Anil. He would like it. I open it. On the very first page, it says, *A true leader seeks to help those who are doing good.*

Doing good. That's Book Uncle. A true leader. Isn't that what Karate Samuel wants to be?

I run to the kitchen and I pick up the phone that now has its ringtone back. I call Anil.

"Anil," I say, "you know everything about Karate Samuel, right?"

"Almost," says Anil. "Why?"

"Do you think he wants to be a true leader?"

"Of course he does," says Anil.

"In that case," I say, "we need to remind him. Are you with me, Anil?"

"Hiya!" Anil yells into the phone. Then he says, "Sorry, Yasmin. I did not mean to hurt your ears. It was just a karate way of saying, Yes, I'm with you."

Karate Samuel did not win this election, I tell myself. Whose victory is it, anyway?

Ours, that's whose. *We* won this election. Now we have to make sure he does not forget Book Uncle.

29

City Hall

TWENTY DAYS AFTER our victory, here
are all the people who go to city hall to
welcome Mayor Karate Samuel as he begins his new job. Me, Reeni, Anil. Anil's
grandmother. My parents. Mrs. Rao. Shoba Aunty and Arvind Uncle. Chinna Abdul Sahib, carrying his number two best
drum, since the very best one is too precious (and also too big) to carry around.
The boy from 2C, his parents and his
grandmother, and their yappy dog. The
newly-marrieds, the school bus driver, the

fruit man and his wife, the istri lady, the istri lady's daughter-in-law, her son, her grandchildren. Six babies and three donkeys. The donkeys belong to relatives of the istri lady. They have come all the way from where they live by the river on the edge of the city.

Very quietly, making no fuss, Book Uncle comes with us.

In Anil's hand is the karate book, which I have given to him. He takes it with him wherever he goes. According to him, you never know when a karate book will come in handy, which makes sense to me.

We arrive at city hall and tell the doorman we want to see the mayor. He seems a bit startled, but he runs in and tells someone.

He comes back and asks, "Do you have an appointment?"

"We are voters," says the istri lady. "Do voters need appointments?"

The doorman disappears once more. Then he returns and tells us to wait.

We wait. Five minutes go by. Ten. Fifteen. Eighteen.

Just in time — that is to say before I explode with impatience — the new mayor himself comes out of city hall.

"My loyal supporters!" he says, flashing his shiny white teeth at us. "Thank you for coming to see me! I have not won this election. *You* have won this election."

He waits for applause.

That is exactly what I thought. *We* won. But now, coming from him, it sounds fake.

There is silence, only breathing, and all of us are waiting, waiting.

I look at Reeni. She looks at Anil. Anil looks at me.

Who is going to take charge?

Anil holds out the karate book. I shake my head in confusion.

"Just take it," he whispers.

So I take it from him, and somehow just having a book in my hand reminds me why we are all here.

I clutch the book very, very tight. I say, my voice so very small in this very big crowd of people, "Mayor Karate Samuel, sir. My name is Yasmin Kader and … and I want you to meet Book Uncle."

Mayor Karate Samuel stares at me as if I have just spoken in some foreign language.

At last he smiles brightly.

"Oh. Yes," he says. "I remember. Something about a library, was it? Yes, yes, Mr. Book Uncle can certainly apply for a non-commercial permit."

I am speechless. Dumbstruck. You could knock me down with a raintree flower!

What? That's all he can say? A non-commercial permit? And how long will that take? How much will it cost?

Was the istri lady right? Now that he is elected, Karate Samuel thinks he can brush us all away. He wants to forget all about us.

30

My Voice

WHAT CAN I do? I have to do something.

I do the only thing I know how to do. I open the book in my hand to page one, and I read out loud.

"A true leader seeks to help those who are doing good."

I read it twice, and suddenly the words are clear and true. The last time I read this book, its words blurred on the page. They made no sense. Now I really understand what Book Uncle means when he says, "The right book for the right day."

Today is the day. This is the book.

So I use my best listen-very-carefully voice. The voice that Mrs. Rao uses when she tells us something really, really important.

"Here are all these people who voted for you because they thought that you would do good. So ... will you ... please tell us ..."

At this point, I am shocked to find that my throat gets tight. This has never happened even once in my life. My hands get sweaty. My listen-very-carefully voice has holes in it. I cannot say another word.

What do I do now? I have no other kind of voice left.

Then, just when I can see that those chickens I counted (too soon) are starting to roll away like lost marbles ...

THAKKA-THAKKA-THAAM-THAAM!

A perfect drumbeat sounds from just behind me.

142

Thakkitta-THAAM! THAKKA-thim-mi-thaaam!

And something magical happens. My voice returns and it is stronger than before, an A-One campaign-perfect, I-mean-it kind of voice. I tell Karate Samuel all about Book Uncle. How he has books for everyone. How he loves each book like a friend, and all he wants to do is share his books with the whole city, with anyone who wants to read one. He can't afford to pay for permits. They will take time. We can't wait for that. We need him back now.

"If you are a true leader," I say, "then you tell me. Why do you have to have a permit in our city to do good things?" And I hold out the karate book.

Mayor Karate Samuel reaches out a hand. He takes the book from me. He opens it. He stares at it. He stares some more. He looks up and stares at me.

If there was a feather handy, I could

have tried it out to see if it worked as a knockdown weapon.

Then the new mayor smiles a slow smile.

I recognize that smile. It is the smile I smile when Book Uncle finds the right book for the right day, just for me.

"A true leader …" Mayor Samuel whispers, and he turn-turn-turns the pages. "You have more like this?" he asks.

Book Uncle folds his hands and tips his head and beams at the mayor through his super-thick glasses.

"Many more," he says.

I nod-nod-nod my head.

The mayor looks at Book Uncle. He looks at me. He straightens up. He takes a breath. We all wait — kids and grown-ups, babies and yappy dog and donkeys — all of us together.

"You, sir," says Mayor Karate Samuel, his best hero voice ringing out, "will get your permit — FREE! It will be issued at once, express-track, I promise you. I will see to it myself."

The crowd goes wild. We roar and cheer, clap, foot-stamp, drum, dog-yap, donkey-bray, baby-babble, sing snatches of songs from Karate Samuel's movies, and shout, "Hiya!"

31

Book Uncle's Place

IN JUST A FEW more days, an even bigger crowd shows up on the corner of St. Mary's Road and 1st Cross Street to celebrate the now officially permitted Book Uncle's Free Lending Library.

There are so many people that the city has to close the road to cars and buses and autorickshaws, bikes and motorbikes and scooters and anything else with wheels.

People and animals are allowed, which is good because Anil has brought his dog, Bubbles. He has also brought the students and the teacher from the karate studio where he takes lessons. They are all wearing their white uniforms with brightly colored belts. Anil's is blue.

All this time I did not know that about him. He is a blue belt.

The istri lady's whole family is here again, along with their three donkeys, who have to be scolded for trying to eat the flowers tucked into Mrs. Rao's hair. A troupe of acrobats has arrived from somewhere. I have never seen them before, but their leader seems to know Book Uncle.

Mayor Karate Samuel cuts a ribbon. Musicians play. Dancers dance. Jugglers juggle. Book Uncle's patrons wander around looking pleased. Acrobats leap over poles. Karate champions block, punch and kick. Mrs. Rao dabs at her eyes with the end of her sari.

She is not sad. She is very, very pleased that we have learned to be such fine citizens. Our school bus driver belts out his

A-One favorite songs from Karate Samuel's movies. He sings them at the top of his voice. We all sing along and clap our hands and stamp our feet in time.

And here is Book Uncle. He cannot stop smiling. He sits in a chair next to his books. They are laid out in perfect stacks. The fruit man and his wife have helped Book Uncle set up this fine new reopened lending library.

Look at the pavement — newly patched! Nice and even. No broken bricks.

And just look at the new and improved sign, relettered and sharpened up.

Books. Free.
Give one.
Take one.
Read–Read–Read.

UMA KRISHNASWAMI is the author of more than twenty books for children, from picture books *(The Girl of the Wish Garden, Bright Sky, Starry City* and *Out of the Way! Out of the Way!)* to novels for young readers *(The Grand Plan to Fix Everything)*. Her books have been published in eleven languages and have been picked for CCBC Choices, Parents' Choice, IRA's Notable Books for a Global Society, the Scientific American Young Readers' Book Award, Bank Street Best Books of the Year and the Paterson Prize. Originally published in India, *Book Uncle and Me* won the Scholastic Asian Book Award and the Crossword Book Award.

Born in New Delhi, Uma teaches at Vermont College of Fine Arts in the MFA program in writing for children and young adults. She lives in Victoria, British Columbia.

umakrishnaswami.org